# Oh, Baby!

For Mandy

Library of Congress Control Number: 2002106373.

ISBN 978-0-448-42704-1          O P Q R S T

# KATIE KAZOO, SWITCHEROO

# Oh, Baby!

by Nancy Krulik • illustrated by John & Wendy

Grosset & Dunlap

# Chapter 1

"So what did *you* do this weekend?" Jeremy Fox asked his best friend, Katie Carew. Katie, Jeremy, and Katie's *other* best friend, Suzanne Lock, were all standing in the schoolyard on Monday morning.

"I taught Pepper to roll over," Katie answered. Pepper was Katie's brown-and-white cocker spaniel.

"Can he do it?" Jeremy asked.

"Yeah. Pepper's real smart," Katie told him. "You just have to give him a treat and he'll do any trick."

"Maybe I should try that with Heather," Suzanne said. Heather was Suzanne's three-month-old sister. "She's been trying for days to roll over. She gets as far as her side and then she flops back down again."

Jeremy laughed. "I guess that means Katie's dog is smarter than your sister," he said.

Suzanne gave Jeremy a dirty look. Then she turned to Katie and smiled brightly. "I had the coolest weekend!" she said.

Katie choked back a giggle. Suzanne said the same thing every Monday morning. "What did you do?" she asked her.

"I went to the mall with my *dad*," Suzanne told her. "You know what *that* means."

"It means you got whatever you wanted," Jeremy said.

Suzanne nodded. "Exactly. That's how it always is with my dad. When he gets into a buying mood, he just shops, shops, shops!"

"My dad *never* gets in a buying mood," Katie sighed. "He hates shopping."

"Mine too," Jeremy agreed. "But I don't like to shop either, so it's okay."

"What did you get at the mall?" Katie asked Suzanne.

Suzanne pointed to her T-shirt. It was white with a big American flag in the middle. The stars were all made of glitter. "I got this shirt. I also got the new Bayside Boys CD. Its called *We're Back!*"

"You're so lucky!" Katie exclaimed. "That CD just came out. I'll bet you're the first one in school to get it."

Suzanne smiled broadly. "Gee, you think so?"

"So, is it any good?" Jeremy asked her.

"Oh yeah!" Suzanne exclaimed. "Even better than the *first* Bayside Boys CD. I was dancing around my room all day yesterday."

Jeremy nodded "I heard the new song on the radio. They're a pretty good group," he agreed.

Suzanne stared at him with surprise. "*Pretty* good?" she demanded. "They're not pretty good. They're the best!"

"I don't know about that," Jeremy said.

"Well, I do," Suzanne argued. "They're the

greatest group in the whole world. Don't you think so, Katie?"

Katie twirled a lock of her red hair around her finger nervously. She hated it when her two best friends disagreed. It always left her stuck in the middle. No matter what she said, someone would be mad.

"I like them a lot," Katie told Suzanne finally. "At least, I liked their first CD. I haven't heard this one yet."

"It's great," Suzanne assured her. "I think everyone should get it. In fact . . ." Suzanne stopped in the middle of her sentence and smiled at Jeremy. "Are all of the articles for this week's *3A Times* written yet? she asked.

Jeremy was the editor of the *3A Times*, the class newspaper. He was the one who asked people to write articles.

"Not yet," Jeremy told Suzanne.

"Good! Suzanne declared. "I want to write about the new Bayside Boys CD. I want to tell everyone how great it is."

Jeremy pulled a small black notebook from his bag. He pushed his wire glasses up on his nose and looked at a list of articles. "Okay," he told Suzanne finally. "I have room for one more story."

"Great!" Suzanne exclaimed. "I'll get started tonight."

As Jeremy put away his notebook, their teacher, Mrs. Derkman, blew a loud whistle. "Class 3A, line up," she called out across the playground.

# Chapter 2

"Hey there, Katie Kazoo," George Brennan said as he walked past her into the classroom.

Katie smiled. Katie Kazoo was the nickname George had given her. When he had first started calling her that, it made her kind of mad. But now she liked being Katie Kazoo. It sounded cool.

"Hi, George," she said.

"So do you know what the rug said to the floor?" George asked Katie.

Katie laughed. That would have seemed like a weird question from anyone else. But Katie knew it was just of one of George's jokes. George *loved* to tell jokes.

"No, what *did* the rug say to the floor?" Katie asked.

"I've got you covered!" George exclaimed. He laughed at his own joke. Katie laughed too.

"If you liked that one, you'll love this one," George continued. "What did one cucumber say to the other cucumber?"

"What?" Katie said.

"If you'd kept your mouth shut, we wouldn't be in this pickle," George told her.

Katie giggled harder. "That one was *really* funny."

"Katie, please find your seat," Mrs. Derkman interrupted.

Katie blushed. Quickly, she scrambled to her desk.

George began to head over toward his desk, too, but Mrs. Derkman blocked his path. "You don't need to sit down, George," Mrs. Derkman said.

"I don't?" George asked.

Mrs. Derkman shook her head. "Since

you're so interested in speaking during class, you can go to the front of the room and give your current-events report."

Usually, George hated when it was his turn to talk about current events. But today he grinned as he pulled a newspaper article from his binder.

"My article is about the movie *Tornado*," he told the class.

Before he could say another word, Mrs. Derkman interrupted him. "That's not really current events, George," she said.

George looked very sad—so sad that Mrs. Derkman said, "Well, why don't you tell us about it anyway?"

George smiled brightly. "*Tornado* just opened this weekend," he began. "It earned almost seventy-five million dollars in ticket sales. That's a lot of money. A lot of people think that it could be the biggest-selling movie of all time. They think it could win a lot of awards, too. All those people are right.

*Tornado* is a great movie. I should know. I saw it with Kevin on Saturday."

*Wow!*

Everyone stared at George and Kevin. It was hard to believe they had been brave enough to go see *Tornado*. The ads on TV looked really scary.

"Any questions?" George asked. You were always supposed to ask for questions at the end of your current-events report.

"Was the movie as scary as it looks on TV?" Mandy Banks asked.

"Scarier," George said proudly.

"Did your parents take you to see it?" Miriam Chan wondered.

"Nope, Kevin's big brother, Ian, took us," George said.

"Did you sit through the whole thing?" Manny Gonzalez asked.

"Of course," George told him.

"Did the tornado look real?" Jeremy asked.

"Totally!" George nodded.

Just then, Mrs. Derkman stood up and walked to the front of the room. "Thank you for that report," she told George. "If any of you have more questions for George or Kevin, you can ask them at lunch. Right now, please take out your math workbooks."

Katie was glad that Mrs. Derkman had
changed the subject. Katie didn't like scary
movies. She was especially afraid of big
winds, like the kind they showed in *Tornado*.
There was a good reason for that. Katie had
been swept up in big winds herself. *Twice*.

And both times her life had really changed.

It had all started on a day when Katie was so sad that she'd wished she could be anyone but herself. There must have been a shooting star in the sky at the time, because Katie's wish came true. The next thing she knew, a big, strong, magic wind was blowing all around her. When the wind stopped, Katie had been turned into Speedy, the class hamster!

Katie changed back into herself pretty fast, but the magic wind wasn't through with her. A couple of days later it blew again . . . turning Katie into Lucille, the lunch lady in the cafeteria. Talk about *awful*. She'd had to serve disgusting cafeteria food!

It had been a few weeks since that last disaster. But Katie was convinced the magic wind would be back. She just didn't know when. And she didn't know who it would turn her into.

That was scarier than any movie could ever be!

# Chapter 3

At lunchtime, everyone tried to sit near Kevin and George. They wanted to hear all about *Tornado*.

"This house gets lifted right up in the air," Kevin said. "And it didn't look fake like that tiny house in *The Wizard of Oz*. It was a real flying house." He took a big bite of his tomato. Tomatoes were Kevin's favorite food.

"I doubt it was a real house," Suzanne argued. "It was probably just some dumb special effect."

"How would you know, Suzanne?" Kevin asked her. "You haven't seen *Tornado*."

Suzanne rolled her eyes. She looked across

the table at where Miriam and Mandy were sitting. "Do you guys want to come over after school to hear the new Bayside Boys CD?" she asked. "I just got it."

Mandy shook her head. "Thanks anyway, but my older sister bought that CD on Friday. She and her friends were playing it all weekend long."

"My brother got it, too," Miriam added. "I probably heard it thirty times yesterday."

Mandy moved closer to George. "Were you scared at the part of the movie when the tornado came near the mall?" she asked him. Suzanne didn't wait for George's answer. She stood up and walked away from the table. Jeremy followed behind her.

"Um, Suzanne, I wanted to talk to you about that Bayside Boys article you were going to write," he said slowly.

"What about it?" Suzanne asked.

"Well, it's just that it seems like everyone has heard the CD already. There's no real

reason to put an article about it in the newspaper," Jeremy told her. "I'm going to ask George and Kevin to write an article about *Tornado* instead."

Suzanne turned away and stormed over to where Katie was sitting. "We need to talk," Suzanne said.

Katie nodded. She took the last bite of her sandwich, then followed Suzanne to the girls' room. Suzanne looked under all the stalls to make sure no one was there. No one was. They were alone.

"We have to see *Tornado*," Suzanne said finally.

"Why?" Katie asked.

"Because George and Kevin have seen it," Suzanne explained.

"So what?" Katie asked.

Suzanne's face was getting red. "We can't let those boys do something we haven't done."

"My mother would never let me see *Tornado*," Katie said.

"Well, you could ask her, couldn't you?"
Suzanne begged. "Katie, I *have* to see that
movie. And I can't go alone."

Katie sighed. She really didn't want to see
*Tornado*, but it seemed so important to
Suzanne. She didn't want to let her friend
down. Still, she didn't want to be scared,
either. No matter what she did, Katie was
going to be unhappy.

So why should Suzanne be unhappy, too?

"Okay," Katie said finally. "I'll ask my mom."

# Chapter 4

"Katie, I just don't think *Tornado* is a movie you should see. You'll get nightmares," Katie's mom explained while she and Katie were sitting in the kitchen having milk and cookies after school.

Katie took a bite of her cookie. "Okay," she said. She chomped down on a chocolate chip. Katie's mother looked at her daughter strangely. She thought Katie would argue with her. But Katie didn't say anything. After all, she didn't really want to see the movie. At least now she could tell Suzanne that she'd tried.

"Can I go over to Suzanne's?" Katie asked.

Her mother nodded. "Be back for supper."

As Katie went outside, Pepper followed
close behind. Together they headed down the
block toward Suzanne's house.

"Hey, wait up!"

Katie turned around to see Jeremy coming
toward her. "What are you doing?" Jeremy
asked her.

"I was just going to Suzanne's," Katie said.
"Wanna come?"

Jeremy shook his head slowly. "She
probably wouldn't want to see me."

"She would if you said you were sorry," Katie told him.

"I guess it wasn't very nice of me to replace her newspaper story with George and Kevin's," Jeremy admitted.

Katie shook her head.

"Maybe I'll come with you and apologize," Jeremy suggested.

Katie smiled. "Good idea," she said.

Suzanne was sitting on her front porch when Katie, Pepper, and Jeremy arrived. She scowled when she saw Jeremy.

"Why is he here?" she asked Katie.

"He wants to apologize," Katie told her.

"I'm sorry, Suzanne," Jeremy said. "It wasn't fair of me to take your article away. I should have made George and Kevin wait until next week. I won't do it again."

Suzanne shrugged and held out her little finger. "Pinky swear?"

Jeremy crooked his finger through hers. "Pinky swear."

But Suzanne still looked sad.

"*Now* what's wrong?" Katie asked her.

"My mother said I couldn't go to see
*Tornado*," Suzanne said. "She said I'm too

young. I am *so* sick of being treated like a baby around here. I'm supposed to be the big one. *Heather's* the baby!"

"*Wah! Wah!*" Just then, baby Heather started crying.

"I have to go see what's wrong," Suzanne said as she stood up. "My mom's doing the laundry," she explained. "I'm supposed to take care of Heather until she's finished."

*Wow!* Suzanne was in charge. Katie was very impressed.

The crying was even louder inside. "What's wrong with her?" Katie asked as she looked down into the playpen. Heather's face was red and covered with tears.

"Maybe she's hungry," Suzanne guessed. "I've got to get her bottle and a baby bib."

"I'll get the bottle," Katie volunteered.

Suzanne shook her head. "Pepper follows you everywhere. If he gets dirty paw-prints on the kitchen floor, my mom will have a fit. She just mopped it."

"So *I'll* get the bottle," Jeremy said.

"Okay," Suzanne said. "It's in the refrigerator. I've got to go upstairs and get her bib."

"*Wah! Wah!*"

Katie was alone with the screaming baby. She covered her ears. Pepper let out a little howl.

Just then, Katie felt a strange wind blow against the back of her neck. She looked towards the front door. Maybe they'd left it open when they'd come inside.

But the door was closed. So were the windows.

*Oh, no!*

This was no ordinary wind. This was the magic wind. And it was getting stronger.

Katie looked over toward Pepper. She wanted to make sure he was safe. But the wind didn't seem to be blowing anywhere near the dog. He was just standing there watching Katie.

Katie was really scared. The wind was big,

powerful, and out of control. But Katie grew even *more* afraid when the wind *stopped* blowing. She knew what that meant.

The magic wind was gone . . . and so was Katie Carew.

# Chapter 5

"RUFF! RUFF! RUFF!"

Pepper's bark rang through the house. It sounded so deep and loud. *That's weird,* Katie thought to herself. *Pepper's never barked like that before.*

"Where am I?" she wondered. "*Who* am I?" Wherever she was, she was lying down. There were thick wooden bars all around her. Katie could see Pepper's face staring at her through the bars. The rest of the room seemed blurry. *Something's wrong with my eyes,* she thought. Katie's ears were working just fine, though. She could hear Pepper loud and clear.

"AROOO!" Pepper howled.

*Too* loud and clear!

Katie's nose was working well, too. Something nearby really stunk. It smelled like the school bathroom at the end of day.

*Blech!* Katie had to get away from that smell. Quickly, she struggled to stand up. But she couldn't seem to climb to her feet. She tried to sit up, but her body wouldn't bend the right way.

Katie couldn't stand. She couldn't sit. She couldn't even roll over to see where she was. All she could do was lie there staring up at the blurry ceiling.

Then, suddenly, something caught Katie's eye. A mobile made of black-and-white animals hung right over her head. Katie watched as the tiny puppies and kittens traveled around and around. It was kind of fun to see them face her and then turn away again.

As she stared at the animals, Katie began to suck on one of her fingers. It calmed her down—until she realized she wasn't sucking on her finger at all. She was sucking on her big toe. *Yuck!*

The bathroom smell was getting really gross. Watching the animals go around was making her dizzy. Pepper's barking was giving her a headache. And now her whole mouth tasted like feet!

It was all too awful. Katie burst into tears.

Suzanne stormed into the room. "Katie, you have to make Pepper stop barking," she said. Then she stopped and looked around. "Katie, where are you?"

Suzanne couldn't see her! Now Katie was really scared. *What if the magic wind made me invisible this time?* she thought.

"Come on, Katie. I know you're here. Quit fooling around," Suzanne called out again.

Katie was afraid to answer her. If Suzanne heard a voice coming from an invisible girl, she'd be really scared. Katie didn't want to scare her friend.

Just then, Jeremy walked into the room. "I've got the bottle," he said.

"Thanks," Suzanne replied. "Have you seen Katie?"

Jeremy shrugged. "No. But she couldn't have gone far. Pepper's still here. "

"That's true." Suzanne agreed.

"Maybe she's in the bathroom," Jeremy said.

Suzanne shrugged. "Maybe. Anyhow, I've got to feed Heather. She's crying again. Pepper's barking is making her nuts."

Suddenly Katie felt something or someone
grab her and lift her off the ground. Katie
looked down. The floor seemed very far away.
Katie couldn't help it. She started crying all
over again.

"Don't cry," Katie heard Suzanne say.

Katie looked up to find a giant Suzanne-head

staring down at her. Her mouth seemed *huge*.

"Here you go," Suzanne said as she shoved a big blob of rubber into Katie's mouth. A sweet, smelly liquid poured out onto Katie's tongue.

"Isn't that yummy, Heather?" Suzanne asked.

*Heather?*

Katie's eyes grew wide with fear. The magic wind hadn't made her invisible. It had turned her into Suzanne's baby sister!

"*WAH!*"

# Chapter 6

"I don't get it," Jeremy said. "I thought that bottle was supposed to make her stop crying."

"So did I," Suzanne agreed. She pulled the bottle from Katie's mouth. "Maybe she's not hungry." Katie wanted to explain to her friends that she wasn't crying because she was hungry. She was crying because she didn't want to be stuck in Heather's tiny body.

But Katie knew she couldn't say anything. She was supposed to be a baby! Babies didn't talk. Suzanne and Jeremy would totally flip out if they knew who this baby really was.

"Let me try one more time," Suzanne said. She shoved the bottle back into Katie's mouth.

Katie made a face and tried to spit the bottle out. But Suzanne held it tight. Katie had no choice. Slowly she began to suck at the smelly, sweet baby formula. As she sucked, she glanced at the clock on the wall. It said 4:45.

Oh, no! Katie's mother had warned her to be home in time for dinner. If the magic wind didn't change her back soon, Katie would be eating baby formula for dinner. And baby formula tasted awful. Katie squirmed and tried to spit the stuff out of her mouth.

"Nope, she's definitely not hungry," Suzanne said finally.

"Then why is she still crying?" Jeremy asked.

"I think she's wet," Suzanne told him. "So what does that mean?"

Suzanne rolled her eyes. "It means we have to change her diaper," she told him.

Jeremy shook his head wildly. "No way!" he declared. "*We* don't have to change her diaper. *You* have to change her diaper. I'm not going near that thing."

"Fine, I'll do it," Suzanne said. She picked up the baby and carried her to the table.

*Oh, no!* Katie thought nervously. Her best friend was about to change her diaper. There was no way that was going to happen!

Katie was so upset, she completely forgot that she was a baby. She opened her mouth and began to scream.

"No, don't!" Katie cried out. She kicked her legs wildly. "Stop!"

Suzanne jumped back with surprise. She looked over at Jeremy. "What did you say?" she asked him.

"I didn't say anything," Jeremy replied. "I thought you did."

"I didn't say anything, either," Suzanne told him.

Jeremy looked at her curiously. "If you didn't say anything, and I didn't say anything, who said that?"

"Stop kidding around," Suzanne told him. "Let me just change the baby and then . . ."

But Katie wasn't going to let that happen. "I said *don't!*" she shouted out again. "I'm fine, guys. There's no wet diaper here. I'm just crying. You know how us babies can be."

Suzanne and Jeremy stared at the baby with amazement.

"Did you hear that?" Suzanne asked Jeremy.

"Uh-huh," Jeremy said slowly.

"Heather talked," Suzanne shouted. "She definitely talked."

"Uh huh," Jeremy said again. He couldn't seem to say anything else.

"But she's only three months old," Suzanne said. "Three-month-old babies can't talk. Unless . . ."

"Unless what?" Jeremy asked her.

"Unless she's a genius!" Suzanne declared. "Heather is the smartest baby in the world!" Suzanne picked the baby up and put her into the playpen. "You stay here," she told Jeremy. "I've got to get my mom!"

As soon as Suzanne was out of the room, Jeremy headed for the front door. He let it slam behind him as he left.

Katie wondered what was so important that Jeremy had to leave right away. But she was glad to be by herself for a few minutes. Well, sort of by herself. Pepper was still in the room with her. The dog walked over to the playpen and stared at Katie.

"I sure hope I turn back into me soon," Katie told her dog. "I can't put off this diaper change thing forever. She squirmed uncomfortably. "I really do think I'm wet in here!"

Pepper barked softly. He knew what it felt like to have an accident.

Just then, Katie felt a familiar breeze begin to blow around Heather's playpen. Katie knew right away that it wasn't an ordinary wind. By now, she could feel the difference between the magic wind and just plain wind. She closed her eyes tight. Katie knew what was going to happen now.

The wind began to blow stronger. The small playpen rocked back and forth wildly. As the wind circled around her, Katie got really scared. The wind was very strong, and she was very small. What if the wind carried her right out of the playpen? Where would she wind up?

Katie gulped. She knew she would never get used to the magic wind. Oh *why* had she ever wished to be anyone other than herself? Right now, she really wished she could be Katie Carew again.

She wanted to be wearing her own clothes—including her dry underpants.

She wanted to be tall enough to look in a mirror and see her own red hair and green eyes.

Katie licked a drip of sticky baby formula from her lip. She wouldn't mind being home in time for dinner, either.

# Chapter 7

"Is this ever going to end?" Katie screamed out as the magic wind circled around her. By now the wind was so strong and loud that she was sure no one could hear her. Katie began to cry as if she *were* a real baby. This was the worst the magic wind had ever been.

And then it stopped—just as suddenly as it had begun. Everything in the room was completely still.

Katie blinked as her eyes focused on a bright white light. It took a minute for her to realize that the light was coming from the ceiling in Suzanne's living room. That was where she'd been before the wind had blown.

And she was still lying flat on her back.

Hadn't the wind changed anything? Was she still baby Heather?

Nervously, Katie looked down toward her feet. Instead of ten tiny toes, Katie saw her bright, red platform sneakers.

"I wouldn't want to put *those* in my mouth," Katie laughed to herself.

Then she looked at her hands. Her fingers were the regular size. The chipped blue nail polish she had forgotten to take off was still there.

No doubt about it. Katie was herself again!

Pepper came over and licked Katie's face. "You knew who I was the whole time, didn't you, boy?" she said as she reached over to pet him. "You're such a smart dog." Pepper licked her face again.

Just then, Katie heard Suzanne's voice. "Honest, Mom, Heather talked to us. She told Jeremy and me not to change her diaper!" Suzanne exclaimed. She practically tripped over Katie as she came into the room.

"Watch it!" Katie called out.

"What are you doing down there?" Suzanne asked her best friend.

"Oh, just lying around," Katie answered nervously as she jumped to her feet. She smiled. It felt good to be standing again.

"Where's Jeremy?" Suzanne asked her.

"I don't know. I guess he left," Katie told her. "He was gone by the time I got back from the bathroom."

Of course, Katie had never actually left

the room. She felt bad about lying to Suzanne, but there was no way Katie could tell her the truth. Suzanne would never believe it anyway.

"Well, you really missed it," Suzanne told Katie. "It was amazing. Heather talked. And not just *goo goo gaa* stuff. She *really* talked."

"Suzanne, I need to get back to the laundry," her mother said. "So if you're finished with this nonsense . . ."

"It's not nonsense," Suzanne insisted. She walked over to the playpen. "I'll bet she'll do it again." Suzanne looked down at her baby sister. "Heather, do you want me to change your diaper?"

Baby Heather stared up at her big sister. She didn't make a sound.

"Come on, Heather," Suzanne urged again. "Are you wet?"

This time, Heather opened her mouth wide.

"Look! She's going to say something!" Suzanne exclaimed.

"WAHHHHHHHH!!!!" Heather let out the

loudest cry Katie had ever heard.

"Well, there's your answer," Suzanne's mother said as she left the room. "She's wet, and she needs her diaper changed."

Suzanne looked like she was about to cry, too. She turned to Katie. "She really did talk," Suzanne insisted. "She *is* the smartest baby ever!"

Katie handed Suzanne a diaper. "I think Heather's really smart . . . even if she doesn't

say another word until she's one year old," she said.

"But that's when *every* baby talks," Suzanne said. "Heather's special."

Katie smiled. "Of course she is," she said kindly. "Just look at who she has for a sister."

# Chapter 8

By the time Katie and Suzanne got to school the next morning, a whole crowd of kids had gathered on the playground. George was the first one to spot the girls coming toward them.

"Hey, Katie Kazoo! Suzanne! Look at this!" he called out. He waved a sheet of white paper high in the air.

"What's that?" Katie asked him.

"The *3A Times*," George told her. "Check it out."

"No, thanks," Suzanne told him. "I've heard enough about *Tornado*."

"Oh, we never wrote that article," George told her. "We forgot."

"Figures," Suzanne said.

"So then what's in the newspaper?" Katie asked George.

"Look!"

Katie took the newspaper from George's hand. Right there, on the front page, was a huge headline. It read:

# SUZANNE'S SISTER SPEAKS!
## Genius baby learns to talk!

Suzanne grinned. "Now, this is what I call news," she said.

Jeremy walked over toward the girls and George. "I wrote the article yesterday after I left your house," he told Suzanne.

Miriam and Mandy raced over to Suzanne.

"What did Heather say, exactly?" Miriam asked.

"Did she really tell you not to change her diaper?" Mandy added.

"Yes!" Suzanne smiled. She really liked all the attention she was getting. "I always knew my sister would be smart, but I never thought she'd be a genius!"

Katie watched as Suzanne talked to the crowd of kids gathered around her. She looked very happy.

"Hey, do you guys know why a mother carries her baby?" George asked the others.

"Why?" Manny asked him.

"Because a baby can't carry her mother!" George answered.

A few of the kids giggled. But most of the class was too busy listening to Suzanne to laugh at George's joke.

Katie could see that George was kind of sad that the kids hadn't thought his joke was really funny. She felt bad for him.

"I liked that one," she whispered to George.

"I can always count on you, Katie Kazoo," George rhymed. "Have you heard this one? Why do moms dress baby girls in pink and baby boys in blue?"

"Why?" Katie asked.

"Because babies can't dress themselves."

Katie giggled. "Very funny."

Just then Mrs. Derkman blew her whistle. It was time to go inside. As the kids lined up, Katie heard Suzanne still talking about Heather.

"Why don't you guys come by after school?" Suzanne said. "Then you can hear Heather for yourselves."

Katie gulped. "Suzanne," she whispered nervously. "I'm not sure that's a good idea."

"Why not?" Suzanne asked.

"Well, you never know. What if Heather doesn't feel like talking again?" Katie said.

"Don't you believe Heather talked?" Kevin asked Katie.

Katie blushed. "Um sure, I guess I do," she said nervously. "But . . ."

"You didn't hear her yesterday," Suzanne told Katie. "I think you're just jealous that you missed it." Suzanne rolled her eyes at Katie. "Can I help it if you're never around when the good stuff happens?"

That made Katie mad! She wasn't jealous at all. She was just trying to keep Suzanne from being embarrassed. Well, if her friend was going act like that, let her bring the other kids home. She'd see.

# Chapter 9

That afternoon, a whole crowd of third graders followed Suzanne home from school. They weren't just kids from Class 3A, either. By the time the end of the day rolled around, almost everyone in the grade had heard about the amazing talking baby.

"You know, I think we should make a videotape of Heather talking," Suzanne told Jeremy as they walked toward Suzanne's house. "She could be on the news."

Jeremy nodded. "She could be famous."

Suzanne looked at the crowd of third graders trailing behind her. "I think she already is."

George and Katie were walking toward the back of the group. "Suzanne seems really happy," George told Katie.

"I guess," Katie said glumly. She knew Suzanne wouldn't be very glad for long.

George studied Katie's frown. "I know how to make you laugh, Katie Kazoo."

George walked over toward Miriam Chan. He opened his mouth wide and pushed on one of his top teeth with his tongue. The tooth wiggled all the way around in a circle. It was really loose.

Miriam made a face. "Eeww! George, that's gross!" she shouted. "Close your mouth."

Katie giggled. Everything grossed Miriam out.

"See, I told you I could make you laugh." George said.

But Katie's laughter didn't last for long. As soon as they reached Suzanne's house, she had that old guilty feeling again. If only she'd told Suzanne about the magic wind, none of this would be happening. But Katie knew she couldn't do that. She couldn't tell anyone.

"You guys wait here," Suzanne said as she went into her house. "I'll bring Heather out."

A moment later, Suzanne came outside again, holding Heather in her arms. "Okay, Heather," Suzanne said. "Say hello to my friends."

Heather looked up at her big sister. "A-goo," she said quietly.

"That's baby talk," Kevin shouted out. "Any baby can do that."

Suzanne shook her head. "She's just warming up," she insisted. "Go ahead, Heather. Say something."

"A-goo," Heather repeated.

"There's nothing special about that baby," Andrew Epstein from Class 3B said, as he and some of his friends left.

"She can't talk," Kevin declared. "Suzanne, you're such a liar."

"I am not!" Suzanne insisted. She looked at Jeremy. "Tell them, Jeremy!"

Jeremy nodded. "She really can talk, you guys. I heard her."

Kevin frowned. "Next time, save it for April Fools' Day."

"Yeah, you should leave the joking to the experts," George added.

"It's no joke," Jeremy insisted. "I wouldn't have written about a joke in the *3A Times*."

"You shouldn't have put this in the paper," Manny said as he walked away. "Mrs. Derkman is going to be so mad!"

Jeremy gulped. If the kids didn't believe them, Mrs. Derkman probably wouldn't, either. He was going to be in big trouble.

Before long, Suzanne, Jeremy, and Katie

were the only ones left standing outside the house. Suzanne looked angrily at Katie. "I'll bet this makes you really happy," she told her.

Katie was really hurt. She never wanted Suzanne and Jeremy to be embarrassed. "No, it doesn't," she insisted.

But Suzanne was too upset to hear her. She took Heather into the house.

Jeremy turned to Katie. "Katie, you believe us, don't you?" he asked. "It had to have been Heather talking. No one else was in the room. Where else could that voice have come from? The bookshelf?"

Jeremy was being silly. But what he said gave Katie a great idea. She knew how to prove that her friends weren't lying—without having to to tell anyone about the magic wind.

"Sorry, Jeremy, I gotta go," Katie said. She raced off down the block.

"Some best friend you are!" Jeremy groaned angrily as he watched her run.

# Chapter 10

The minute she got home, Katie darted upstairs to her room. "Don't you want a snack?" her mother called after her.

"No, thanks," Katie shouted back. "I've got too much to do."

Katie spent the rest of the afternoon in her room working on her plan to save Jeremy and Suzanne. She didn't even want to take the time to eat dinner, but her mother made her.

"You must have an awful lot of homework," Katie's mother said as she piled stir-fried tofu and broccoli onto Katie's plate. Katie's mom and dad were both having meat-loaf, but Katie was a vegetarian. She had decided a few months ago that she was never, ever going to eat anything that had had a face.

Katie shrugged and shoveled her food into her mouth. She chewed as fast as she could. "There! All done," Katie said, showing her parents her empty plate. "May I be excused?"

Katie's mother looked surprised. Usually Katie had to be forced to finish her broccoli. (Just because she was a vegetarian didn't mean she loved *every* vegetable!)

"It was very good," Katie assured her mom.

"I'm glad. I guess you can be excused."

"Thanks!" Katie yelled as she ran back up the stairs toward her room.

"This plan had better work," she said to Pepper as she flopped down and opened the big book on her bed. "It's the only chance Suzanne and Jeremy have."

The next morning, as Katie arrived at school, she saw Suzanne and Jeremy standing by themselves on the blacktop. Suzanne was

kicking angrily at the ground. Jeremy kept fiddling with his glasses.

A bunch of other kids were standing by a tree, pointing at Jeremy and Suzanne. Katie walked right past her two best friends, and joined the group of giggling third graders.

"Man, those two are such jerks!" Kevin declared.

"Yeah, they were just jealous that you got to see *Tornado*," Mandy told him.

"They're big liars," Miriam added.

"Maybe they're not lying," Katie interrupted.

All the other kids stared at her.

"Give me a break," Manny declared. "Just because they're your best friends doesn't mean you have to take their side, Katie. Heather can't talk."

"I know," Katie agreed. "But that doesn't mean they didn't hear her say something."

Manny looked around. "Huh?" he asked. "That's impossible."

"Wanna bet, wise guy?"

Manny looked around some more. "Who said that?" he demanded.

"I did."

"Who said *that*?" Manny repeated.

"*Hello*! Down here!"

George looked down. "I think it's coming from your backpack," he said.

"Yeah, right," Manny said. He turned to see if anyone was standing behind him.

"Don't turn your back on me," the voice said. "I want to see your face for a change."

That made George laugh. "Hey, that's pretty good. Get it? A backpack *always* faces your back!"

Now Manny was confused. "Backpacks can't talk," he insisted. But he stared down toward his pack anyway.

"It sure sounds like your backpack was talking to you, Manny," Katie said.

"That's impossible," Manny declared. "There's no one in there."

"Come see," the voice said. "Take a peek inside!"

Now Manny was getting nervous. So were the other kids.

"Go check the backpack," Katie said sweetly.

"Not me," Manny replied in a small, scared voice.

"Why?" Katie asked him. "Are you chicken?"

Manny didn't answer.

"I'll check it," George said bravely. "Come on, Kevin."

Kevin shook his head. "Leave me out of this," he said. "That backpack's haunted or something."

Katie started to laugh. "You guys are such babies," she said.

She bent down and unzipped the pack. George stood beside her and looked inside. "Nothing in here but your lunch and your math worksheet," he assured Manny. "Ooh. I think you got number five completely wrong!"

Manny blushed. "See, I told you there was no one in there," he said.

"But the the backpack was talking, right?" Katie asked Manny. "You heard it."

Manny nodded slowly.

"Or at least you *thought* you heard it," Katie added. "Just like Jeremy and Suzanne thought they heard Heather talk."

"This is different," Manny said. "I really did hear the backpack talk. We all did."

Katie started to laugh. "Nope. You heard me talk," she said. "That's *my* voice."

"No way," Kevin told her. "You weren't talking."

"Yes, I was," Katie insisted. "I was talking without moving my lips. I made it *seem* like the voice was coming from the backpack. But it was really coming from me."

"Wow!" George exclaimed.

"It's called ventriloquism," Katie continued. "I played the same trick on Jeremy and Suzanne. It wasn't Heather talking. It was me."

Katie bit her lip. That wasn't a *complete* lie. She really was talking for Heather that afternoon. Of course, that's because she had *been* Heather.

"Wow!" George exclaimed. "That's so cool. How did you learn to to do that?"

"My mother bought me a book on ventriloquism for Christmas last year. I've been practicing forever to get it right."

"Can you do some more?" Miriam asked.

Katie smiled. "Sure."

For the next few minutes Katie made Mandy's math notebook whisper, George's sneaker sing, and Miriam's pocketbook cry.

"I guess we owe Jeremy and Suzanne an apology," Kevin admitted. Katie watched from far away as the other kids went over to talk to Suzanne and Jeremy. Suzanne glanced over at Katie angrily. Jeremy was so mad he wouldn't even look in her direction.

Katie was suddenly very glad she'd learned ventriloquism. It seemed like she was going to be spending a lot of time talking to herself.

# Chapter 11

At lunchtime, Katie sat all by herself in the back of the cafeteria. But Suzanne found her anyway. She came storming over with a really angry look on her face.

"I can't believe you did that to us!" Suzanne shouted at Katie.

"I'm sorry," Katie apologized. "But I did warn you not to bring everyone to hear Heather talk."

"Oh, I'm not mad about that," Suzanne told her. "I'm totally over it. All the kids know I wasn't lying."

Katie looked surprised. "You're really over it?"

"Sure. But I'm still mad at you."

"Why?" Katie asked.

"I thought we were best friends. We're supposed to tell each other everything."

Katie gulped. Had Suzanne found out her secret? Did she know about the magic wind?

"How come you didn't tell me you were a ventriloquist?" Suzanne demanded. "We could have been playing tricks on people all this time."

Katie smiled. *What a relief.* Suzanne didn't know about the wind after all. "I practiced my ventriloquism all last night. I wanted it to be perfect today," Katie told her.

"It worked," Suzanne told her. "Everyone was totally impressed."

"Then you're really not upset with me?" Katie asked.

Suzanne shrugged. "Nah. I guess it was a pretty funny joke. Besides, you're the one who had to go tell Mrs. Derkman that you fooled Jeremy into writing a fake article for the *3A Times.*"

"That *was* pretty awful," Katie admitted. "Mrs. Derkman was really angry."

"What's your punishment?" Suzanne asked.

"She's making me write a one-page report about some old ventriloquist named Edgar Bergen."

Suzanne wrinkled her nose. "Extra homework!" she declared. "That's *really* bad."

Just then, Jeremy walked over. "Hey, guys," he said as he put down his tray. He looked curiously at Katie. "How come you're sitting all the way over here?"

Katie blushed and stared at the floor. "I figured you'd be mad at me," she said.

Jeremy nodded. "I was. But I'll forgive you . . . if you do something for me."

"Anything," Katie told him.

"Teach me how to be a ventriloquist. I know a few people I want to play tricks on!" Jeremy said.

Katie grinned. "It's a deal."

"I can't believe I didn't know you could do that," Jeremy said.

Katie thought about all the times the magic wind had turned her into someone else: Speedy the hamster. Lucille the lunch lady. Baby Heather.

"I guess there are a lot of things you guys don't know about me," she admitted finally.

"Like what?" Suzanne asked.

Katie grinned. "That's for me to know and for you to find out!" she teased. Then she looked down at Jeremy's sandwich.

"Aren't you gonna eat me?" the sandwich seemed to say.

"Hey, that's really good!" Jeremy admitted. "Show me how you did that."

As Katie gave her two friends their first ventriloquism lesson, she felt happy inside. It was nice to have things back to normal again.

*At least for a little while.*

# Talk Like Katie!

*Here are some of the ventriloquism tricks that Katie taught Jeremy and Suzanne. Practice them at home. Then see if you can fool your friends!*

It's easy to say these letters without moving your lips: A, C, D, E, G, H, I, J, K, L, N, O, Q, R, S, T, U, X, Y, Z. But most words have other sounds in them, too. Like the letter B—you can't say *that* without moving your lips, can you?

So just how do ventriloquists say words like "banana" or "bubble"? Here's their secret: instead of making a B sound, they use a D sound. The trick is to quickly slur over the D sound so it sounds sort of like a B.

These are some other ventriloquist tricks:

*To say a word with a P sound, use a T sound instead.

*If you want to say the letter F, make a TH sound, like the one you hear in "thanks."

*If you need to make a V sound, say TH like in the word "there."

*To make a W sound, try using an OO sound, like in the word "boot."

Just remember, it will take a while before the words sound right. It takes a lot of practice to learn to talk without moving your lips. Try to practice in front of a mirror. That way you can see how well you're doing.

When you're ready, try putting on a

ventriloquist show! Any puppet will do—even a sock puppet. (Just wash the sock first. Nobody wants a sock puppet that smells like feet!)

If you're making your puppet speak, be sure to look right at him. That way it will seem like the puppet is talking, not you. If you make your puppet tell a joke, be sure to laugh when the audience does. After all, the joke was funny, wasn't it?

Here are some of George Brennan's favorite jokes. You can use them in your act, or you can make up a few of your own.

*What cat can't you trust?*
A cheetah!

*What's the difference between the North Pole and the South Pole?*
The whole world!

*What's the difference between here and there?*
The letter T!

*Why did the rooster run away from the fight?*
Because he was chicken!

*Why do hummingbirds hum?*
Because they don't know the words!